ST. BERNARD
DOBERMAN PINSCHER
DACHSHUND

First published in the United States of America in June 2023 by "Clever-Media-Group" LLC
www.clever-publishing.com

ISBN 978-1-956560-41-1 (hardcover)

For information about permission to reproduce selections from this book, write to:

CLEVER PUBLISHING
79 MADISON AVENUE; 8TH FLOOR
NEW YORK, NY 10016
USA

For general inquiries, contact: info@clever-publishing.com
CLEVER is a registered trademark of "Clever-Media-Group" LLC

To place an order for Clever Publishing books, please contact The Quarto Group:
sales@quarto.com • Tel: (+1) 800-328-0590

Art created with pencil and Adobe Photoshop
Book design by Katerina Belyaeva
MANUFACTURED, PRINTED, AND ASSEMBLED IN CHINA

10 9 8 7 6 5 4 3 2 1

I WANT TO BE YOUR PUPPY!

by
ELENA ULYEVA

illustrated by
MARY KOLESS

CLEVER
Publishing

David had a birthday coming up. He was going to be five years old! When Mommy and Daddy asked him what he wanted for his birthday, his answer was always the same: a puppy.

But they always said no. “Puppies are a lot of work, David,” Daddy told him.

“But I’m almost five!” David replied. “I know how to take care of a puppy!”

He even got up early on his birthday and drew a picture of the puppy that he wanted.

At his party, David had a yummy birthday cake with a big “5” on the top. And of course, he wondered if he would finally get a puppy.

WILL I GET a PUPPY THIS YEAR?

When it was time for presents, David opened the big one from Mommy and Daddy first. It looked just the right size to have a dog inside!

He looked in the box and saw…a dog! Only it was a stuffed animal, not a real dog.

David was so sad. "I really want a real dog," he told Mommy and Daddy.

"I PROMISE I'LL TAKE CARE OF IT."

REAL DOGS!

Mommy and Daddy talked it over, and they decided to get a dog for the family.

They went to the animal shelter in town. There were so many dogs to choose from!

SO MANY DOGS!

David saw a girl leaving the shelter with a new pet.
I hope I find a puppy for me, too, he thought.

I HOPE WE BECOME FRIENDS FOREVER!

A volunteer at the animal shelter saw David and asked what kind of dog he wanted.

"A cute one!" David said excitedly.

"I think I have the perfect puppy for you," said the man. "I found this puppy outside the shelter. She was all alone and hungry, so we took her inside."

The man handed David the puppy. “Take good care of her,” he said.

“YOU’RE NOW THE MOST IMPORTANT PERSON IN HER LIFE!”

David smiled, and the puppy licked his cheek.

"Do you have everything you need to take care of a puppy?" the man asked.

"Yes!" David said excitedly. He'd wanted a dog for so long, so he knew exactly what he needed—a collar, a leash, food and water bowls, and toys.

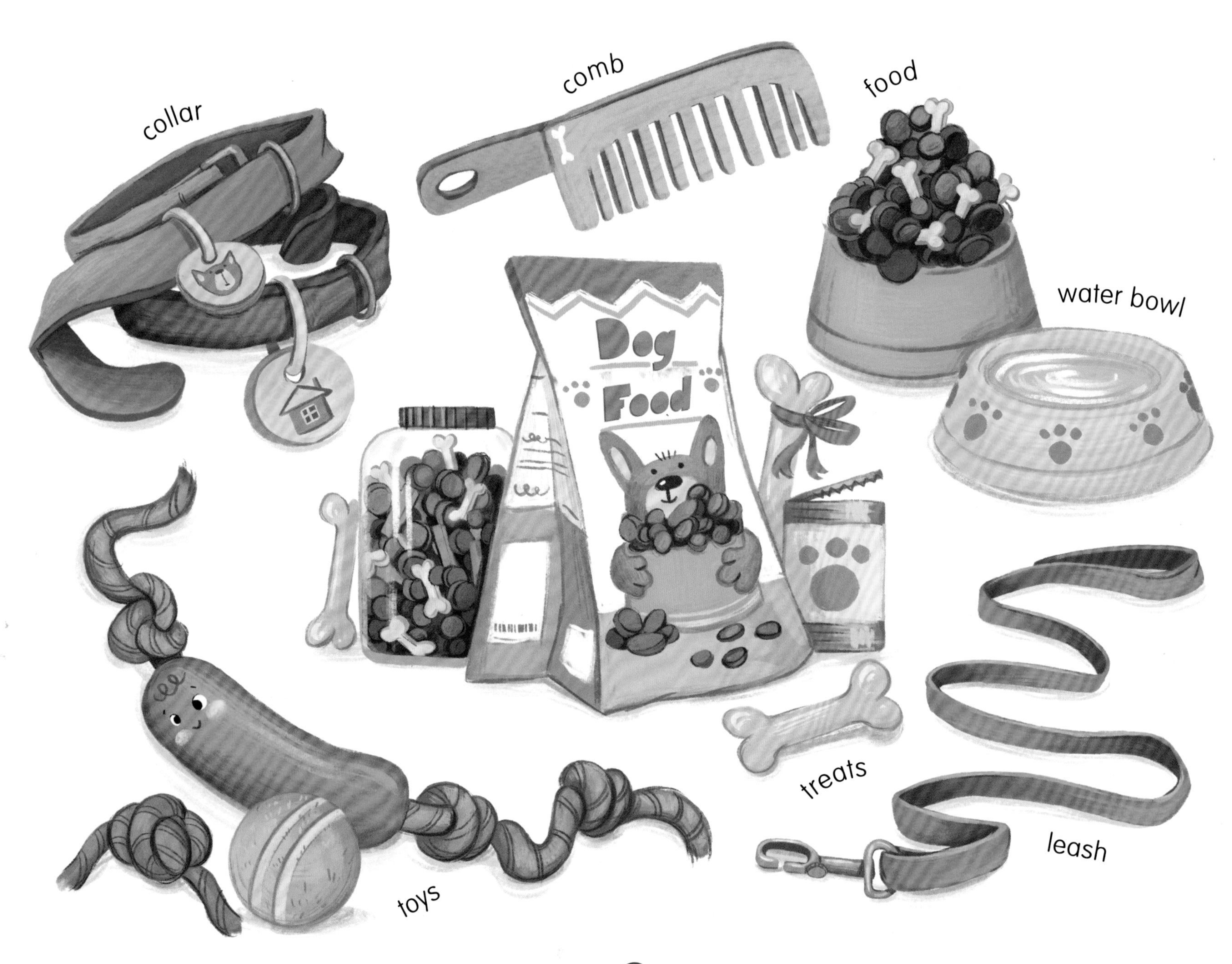

PENNY!

David and his parents took the puppy home. David decided to name her Penny.

YOUR NAME WILL BE PENNY!

The next day, David took Penny to the dog park. There were other dogs running, climbing, fetching, and jumping through hoops.

"Jump!" David told Penny.

COME ON! DO IT!

But Penny didn't jump. She just looked at David and wagged her tail.

"Speak!" David tried again.

Penny continued to smile and wag her tail.

YOU CAN DO IT!

Back home, David tried to show Penny
where she could and couldn't go in the yard.

And when he tossed a ball to her and told her to "Fetch!" she just chewed it and batted it into the air with her paws.

David was upset. Penny wouldn't do what he wanted at all! He decided to bring her back to the animal shelter.

NOT GOOD!

“What’s wrong?” the volunteer asked.
“She won’t do what I want her to do,”
David replied. “She’s not a good puppy.”

NOT GOOD!

David continued, “When I tell her to sit, she does a somersault. When I tell her to fetch, she juggles the ball with her back paws.”

The man thought for a moment. “Not many dogs can do a somersault,” he said. “Or juggle. It sounds to me like your dog does things differently, in her own special way.”

David thought about what the man said and decided to give Penny another chance. After all, she was his special dog!

Before they left, David tossed a ball to Penny, then another, and a third. Soon, she was juggling three balls at once!

David couldn't wait to show his friends what Penny could do. They came over to his house to watch Penny the Amazing Puppy do tricks.

They wanted him to teach their dogs how to do tricks, too!

That night, David hugged Penny tightly. "You're the best puppy in the world!" he told her. "I love you to the moon and back."

Penny licked David on the cheek. She loved him just as much!

A LOVING FAMILY IS THE BEST GIFT!

David realized that Penny was the perfect puppy — even if she did things a little differently!

BEST FRIENDS FOREVER!

HOW TO TAKE CARE OF YOUR FURRY FRIEND

Feed her healthy food.

Brush her teeth.

Give her plenty of water.

Brush her fur.

Have the vet trim her nails.

Clean her ears.
(Be sure to ask a grown-up to help you!)

Give her a bath.

DOGS COME IN ALL SHAPES AND SIZES, AND ALL DOGS ARE SPECIAL!